Vanilla, Chocolate, and Caramel

Story by
Margaret Clyne

Illustrations by
Penny Azar

Michael's grandma lived in a large, old farmhouse in the country. She had a big, white, fluffy cat named Vanilla that was named after her favorite flavor of ice cream.

She also had a big, dark brown rabbit with floppy ears named Chocolate because Grandma really liked chocolate.

One day Michael and his mother decided to drive
out to the country to visit Grandma.
"I'm bringing caramels for Grandma because I know
how much she loves them," said Michael. "What are
you going to bring?"

Mom just smiled and said, "I don't know. We'll see."

They got in their car and headed down the congested
freeway. After what seemed like a very long half hour,
they finally turned on to the long country road leading
to Grandma's house.

They hadn't gone far when Mom spotted a roadside stand. "Look at that, Michael. We can buy some strawberries for our dessert tonight at Grandma's." And so they stopped and bought a carton of juicy strawberries.

A little farther down the road, Mom saw another sign. "They sell fresh cream here, Michael. Let's buy some to go with the strawberries."

After a few more miles, there was a sign advertising fresh produce. "Look, Michael. We can buy some lettuce and tomatoes to make a salad for tonight's dinner." They chose some juicy, ripe tomatoes and a head of crisp lettuce.

Picked this morning!

Best lettuce!

Big, Red and juicy

They were almost at Grandma's when Michael shouted, "Stop, Mom. Look at that! We can buy Grandma a new puppy."

Mom pulled into the driveway and parked the car. She had barely shut off the car before Michael flung open the door and raced across the farmyard.

In a basket, Michael saw three puppies—a black one, a black-and-white one, and a light brown one. Michael picked up the light brown one. "Look, Mom," squealed Michael. "This one is the same color as the caramels we've brought for Grandma! This is the puppy for her."

When they got to Grandma's, they gave her the strawberries for dessert, the cream for the strawberries, and the lettuce and tomatoes for the salad. Then Michael gave her the puppy.

"I have a great idea!" exclaimed Michael. "I think you should name the puppy Caramel, because you like caramels so much." Then he gave her the caramels he had brought for her.

7

After dinner they all played with Vanilla,
Chocolate, and Caramel.

"Now you have all your favorites, Grandma,"
said Michael.

"I certainly do," Grandma said with a smile.